Timmy Trolley Bus' House
School
Bluebell Wood
Dangerous Potatoes
Beware.
Wiggley Windey Road
Monkeyman's Garage
Squinkle's house
Sweet shop
Wika Waka's house
Police Station.
Jail

Story Three

Monkeyman

Chapter 1

Monkeyman

If you're a 'clever clogs,' and think you know everything in the whole wide world, well, I've got a surprise for you. You don't! You probably think that anyone with a name like 'Monkeyman,' would have to be a monkey, or a man, or both! Monkeyman of course, is neither. She is a very clever, pixie-faced little girl, who always does her homework and doesn't look anything like a monkey actually. So there! Clever clogs.

She has beautiful long plaits, a little turned up nose and a big flippy, floppy, fluffy hat, with a wide brim. And the biggest, prettiest, blue eyes you've ever seen. She's never silly or naughty, and she always says thank-you. So, what do you think about that clever clogs?

Monkeyman was in her workshop, welding pieces of metal together into very strange and unusual shapes, when Squinkle came by to see if she wanted to go and get an ice-cream.

"I have to finish what I'm doing first," said Monkeyman.
"What are you doing?" enquired Squinkle.
"That horrible boy Timmy-Trolley-Bus loosened the front wheel on my trike, which made me crash into Bluebell Wood," explained Monkeyman. "And now I'm making something very special, so I'll be able to go into Bluebell Wood, and get my trike without being bitten by the Dangerous Potatoes."

"Oh!" said Squinkle, looking confused. "So when do you want to get an ice cream then?" he asked.

"Look," said Monkeyman, getting a little impatient with him. "You go and get us an ice-cream from the shop, and when you get back I'll have finished my jobs, and then we can eat our ice cream, OK?"

"OK!" replied Squinkle, still looking confused. Monkeyman got back to her banging and bashing and welding.

Squinkle strolled along without a care in the world. Unfortunately Timmy-Trolley-Bus was outside the shop, with his dog Dung Heap, when Squinkle got there.

"Hello Stinkle!" said Timmy-Trolley-Bus.

"I'm not talking to you," said Squinkle. "You made my friend crash her trike in Bluebell Wood."

"Yeah, and that means she lost the race," sneered Timmy-Trolley-Bus.

"So!! Who cares about your silly race? We're going to get her trike back, and then she'll beat you fair and square," said Squinkle angrily.

"Oh, but what about the Dangerous Potatoes?" asked Timmy-Trolley-Bus sarcastically. "They'll bite her on the bottom if she goes in Bluebell Wood."

"She's making something, I don't know what it is, but she's making something very special, then she won't get bitten. So there!!" said Squinkle. With that he turned around and marched into the shop to buy ice-cream for himself and Monkeyman.

"I wonder what she's making?" thought Timmy-Trolley-Bus. "I must find out." Just then, Squinkle came out of the shop carrying two huge delicious looking ice-creams that were nearly as big as him.

"Give me a lick!" demanded Timmy-Trolley-Bus.

"NO! Get your own!" shouted Squinkle.

"OK," said Timmy-Trolley-Bus. "You can have both of them all to yourself." And, as Squinkle turned to walk away, Timmy-Trolley-Bus grabbed both of the ice-creams and squashed them upside down on poor Squinkle's head!

Chapter 2

Metal Pants

Monkeyman couldn't believe her eyes when she looked up from her welding.

"Oh my goodness," she gasped as poor Squinkle trudged miserably into the garage, with cold sticky ice-cream dripping down his face and the two cones stuck to the top of his head like horns.

"Timmy-Trolley-Bus?" she asked knowingly. Squinkle just nodded his head sadly.

"He's getting worse," said Monkeyman. Squinkle nodded his head some more. "I think we might just need to teach him a lesson pretty soon," she said. Squinkle kept on nodding.

Just then Wika Waka turned up at Monkeyman's garage. He looked at Squinkle strangely and said, "Timmy-Trolley-Bus?" Both Monkeyman and Squinkle nodded their heads silently.

"You know what?" said Wika Waka. "We're going to have to teach him a lesson pretty soon."

They both looked expectantly at Monkeyman, who always knew what to do, and how to do it.

"Yes. But first we have a job to do," she said. "We need to go to Bluebell Wood and get my trike back."

"What about the Dangerous Potatoes?" asked Wika Waka. "You know they'll bite you on the bottom."

"Not if I'm wearing my metal pants!" exclaimed Monkeyman proudly.

"*WHAT?*" chorused the two boys together! Then, with a flourish, Monkeyman

Dangerous potatoes

Acknowledgements

To my wife Ann, thank you for saving my life.

My eldest daughter Lula, the original Monkeyman.

My boys and girls Jake, Callum, Olivia and Willow
for listening in wide eyed amazement.

My sister Jackie and my nephews Sean and Simon
for Easter egg hunts in Bluebell wood, (In the day time of course).

Mark, Joanne, Samuel and Toby for help with the finer details.

Special thanks to Roger King for pointing out my over use of the lowly comma
and Sarah Kershaw for relighting the fire

This book is born out of bedtime stories.

Never stop telling them.

Nick Beggs

Cover colouring and layout Steve Cripps

Editing and proof reading Mark Webb and Adrienne Staniford

Published by Diverze Publishing - www.diverze-publishing.com

First Edition - Printed 2012 in Great Britain by Diverze Print - www.diverze-print.com

Foreword

Some children don't like soggy cabbage, smelly sprouts or bitter broccoli but, of course, everyone loves potatoes. They are just delicious chipped, roasted, mashed or fried. Unless, they happen to be Dangerous Potatoes! (Solanum Tuberosum Periculosum.)

"How can a potato be dangerous?" I hear you ask. Well, if you've never seen a Dangerous Potato you're very lucky. The children in this book weren't quite so lucky! But, you'll have to read the stories to find out just how dangerous potatoes can be!

Oh, but before you get started there's one more thing you need to know about Dangerous Potatoes. They can change nature around themselves. They can turn normal things into unusual things, because they are freaks of the vegetable world. And beware. Even listening to stories about Dangerous Potatoes can make strange things happen to you. However, the truth is, Dangerous Potatoes just want to be left alone and it's only when people bother them that problems begin. But isn't all of nature like that?!!!

The problems were only just about to begin for the children who lived in a strange sleepy little town, but for your own safety it's best you don't know where it is. No, I'm not going to tell you just incase you are tempted to go there and search for Dangerous Potatoes yourself. That would be asking for trouble. What I will say is it's a small picturesque little English town with wiggly, winding roads that amble between pretty, well-kept gardens. It's a bit of an old-fashioned place with lots of things left over from the olden days... Days which your mummy and daddy may remember. So if anything seems very old and strange in this book, just ask your parents.

Meanwhile here's a map of the town to get you started.

pulled a big dusty old sheet away to reveal what did indeed look like... metal pants!

"*WHAT?*" asked the boys again; still not able to understand exactly what she was showing them!

"Well don't just stand there staring at me," said Monkeyman. "Turn around while I put them on, and *no* peeking."

The boys looked at each other, then turned around to face the other way while bangs and bashing noises emanated from behind them as Monkeyman wrestled to put on the metal pants. BANG... BASH... BOING... TINKLE.... JANGLE ..... AARROOOHA....... POINK..... What a racket! The boys couldn't believe their ears.

"OK, you can look now," said Monkeyman, slightly out of breath. There before them stood this pretty little girl, wearing a huge pair of ugly metal pants, with bolts and screws and rivets all over them.

"I don't think they suit you at all," said Squinkle.

Wika Waka elbowed him in the ribs and said, "They're not a fashion statement, dummy, they're for protection."

"That's right," replied Monkeyman. "Now let's get to Bluebell Wood and find my trike." Then off they all hurried on their mission, chatting as they went and marvelling at the metal pants. Even Monkeyman was oblivious of Timmy-Trolley-Bus following behind, at a safe distance so he wouldn't be spotted. "I wonder what they're up to," he thought to himself as he crept along behind.

It wasn't long before the three pals found themselves back at Bluebell Wood. The sun shone through the trees, the birds sang, and bluebells lay before them like a deep blue carpet.

"It looks like a different place during the day time," said Wika Waka.

"Yes. It's hard to believe there are Dangerous Potatoes in there at all," said Squinkle.

"Oh they're there alright," replied Monkeyman. "We've seen them."

"So what are we doing exactly?" enquired Squinkle.

"Just lay down here in the grass so if they try to bite me, they won't see you," said Monkeyman. Anyway, they can't come out of the wood, they don't like the light." Then she walked calmly into the wood. Nobody saw a certain very naughty boy hiding up a tree to get a good view of what was happening.

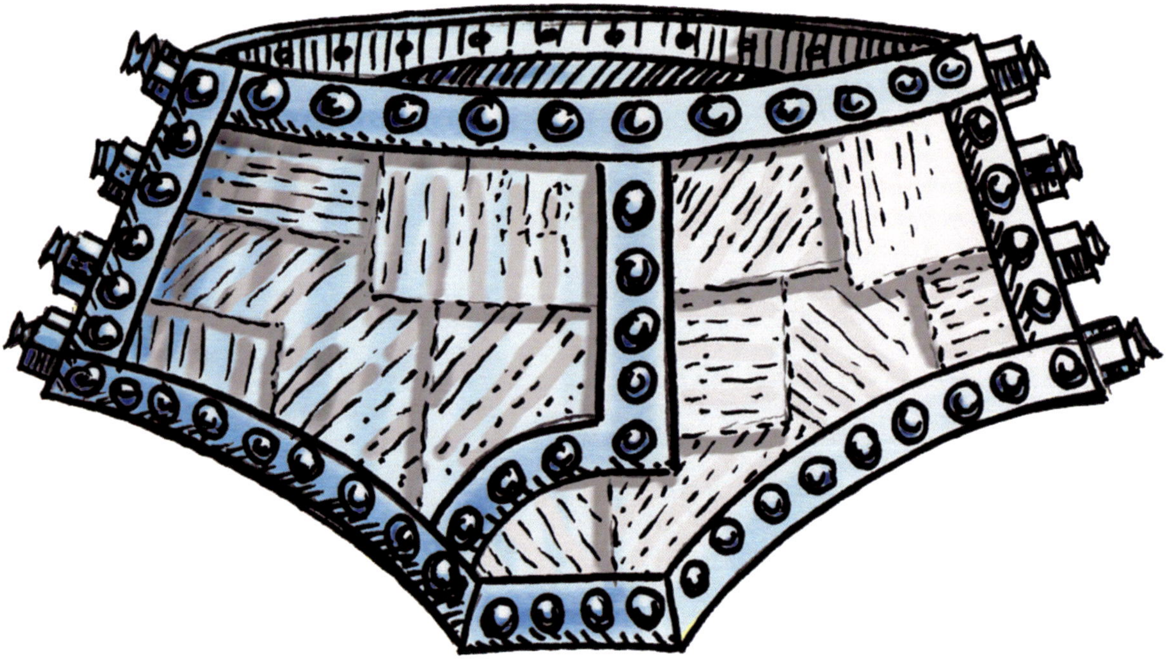

Chapter 3

The Tree-House Stake-Out

It didn't take Squinkle and Wika Waka very long to work out that Dangerous Potatoes don't come out during the day. However, up to that point, they had all been utterly terrified by the memory of Monkeyman being chased out of Bluebell Wood by hundreds of hungry vegetables. To lighten the mood, and bring some relief to the tense situation, Monkeyman did a funny dance for the boys. This involved wiggling her metal bottom around, looking down at the ground and shouting "Dinner is ready you stinky Potatoes.... Come and get it, come and get it while it's hot!"

Wika Waka and Squinkle rolled around in the bluebells laughing and they didn't notice the time passing quickly. Finally they got bored with that game and Monkeyman said, "Well, we still haven't found my trike and it will be dark soon, so I think we should build a tree-house for safety."

"Great!" said Wika Waka. "Cool idea."

"Oh no!" said Squinkle "How are we going to do that?"

"Just like this," said Monkeyman, and she started running around collecting pieces of dead wood that lay on the ground between the bluebells. Wika Waka quickly joined in. Slowly Squinkle got the idea, and started to help out as well. Timmy-Trolley-Bus kept quiet, and watched from his treetop hide- out.

Soon, thanks to Monkeyman's clever planning and some hard work by all of them, the children had finished building the coolest tree-house you have ever seen.

It had a rope ladder, as well as a special crane for pulling Monkeyman's trike up to safety.

"Now, maybe we can get on with the job of finding my trike," said Monkeyman. "It'll be dark soon, and we know that the Dangerous Potatoes will be out."

"Well, we can't help you," said Squinkle. "We don't have any metal pants."

"I know that," said Monkeyman, "but you can stay here and guard the tree-house until I get back." And off she clunked in her metal pants. The boys climbed up the rope ladder into the tree-house, and watched as Monkeyman wandered off into the wood.

It was indeed getting dark now, and Timmy-Trolley-Bus had been watching everything! "I want to play in that tree-house, and have it for myself," he thought. So he crept quietly, and stealthily, along the branch of the big tree he had been hiding in until he was dangling directly over the tree-house. In the gloom, Squinkle and Wika Waka couldn't see him above them, and continued keeping a look out for Monkeyman.

Chapter 4

Potato Attack

Monkeyman, meanwhile, was shuffling her way through the bluebells looking for her trike. This was very difficult as it was dark all around, and spooky noises filled the air. But Monkeyman is a determined, brave little girl and she just kept on searching high and low. At one point she thought she had found it under a pile of leaves but, when she pulled it up, she could see it was only a rusty old pram. "Oh no," she said grimly, "I'll never find it in the dark." Pausing for a moment, she looked off in the distance to where the moon was shining brightly through the trees.

"That's where it is," she said to herself. And indeed that's where it was, lying down next to a big tree in the moonlight. "Thank you Mr. Moon," whispered Monkeyman, as she got up and marched towards her trike.

She was almost skipping as she went, and she didn't notice the beady eyes peering at her from beneath the ground.

"Heeee Heeee Heeee." It was the squeaky cackle of potato voices. Immediately Monkeyman stopped in her tracks, lifted her arms in the air and stared at the ground.

"Oh no, not Dangerous Potatoes, not now when I've found my trike," she said. Slowly, she crept over the peering angry eyes, towards her beloved trike.

All of a sudden, one of the potatoes sprang up out of the ground, and tried to bite her on the bottom. ‘BOINK,’ it went, as it bounced off the metal pants. Then three more tried. ‘BOINK,’ ‘BANG,’ ‘BASH,’ went the potatoes as they bounced off the metal pants. Monkeyman started to run as fast as she could towards her trike, which just made the potatoes angrier. Hundreds of them leapt from the ground and tried to bite her with their big white gnashing teeth, but of course they couldn’t. Every time they tried, they either bounced off or broke their teeth on her metal pants. But Dangerous Potatoes never give up. They just kept coming, ‘BOINK’, ‘BASH’, ‘BANG’, ‘BEEOING’, went the Dangerous Potatoes.

Monkeyman neared her trike, and reached down to pick it up. One of the potatoes bit her hand, another bit her ear. “Aw, get off you smelly potatoes,” she shouted, starting to get angry now. Quickly she sprang onto her trike, and pedalled furiously through the sea of bouncing, barking Dangerous Potatoes. Some of them got squashed as Monkeyman rode over the top of them, showering her face and fluffy hat with mashed potato. SPLOSH, SPLONG, SPLAT.

“I hope the boys have got the crane ready to lift me up into the tree-house,” she thought, out of breath now but riding ever faster.

But what was this? As she approached the safety of the tree-house, she was shocked to see Squinkle and Wika Waka running around on the ground, trying to get away from yet more Dangerous Potatoes! She looked up at the tree-house, only to see Timmy-Trolley-Bus pointing and laughing hysterically at their predicament.

“He crept up on us when we weren’t looking, and threw us out of the tree-house,” shouted Squinkle, as he spied Monkeyman coming towards them. “What are we going to do?” he pleaded.

Chapter 5

Mashed Potatoes

"Get on my trike!" ordered Monkeyman. As quick as he could, Squinkle ran and jumped on Monkeyman's back, as she rode closer to the tree-house.

Wika Waka meanwhile was running around in circles, trying to escape the potato attack.

"Aw, get off. Ouch, ooh, eeeh, go away," he shouted. Then he fell over a big stick, and the Dangerous Potatoes were upon him. Biting his nose, his ears, his chin and of course...... his bottom.

"AAAAAAAAWWWWWWWWHHHHH," wailed Wika Waka. He picked up the big stick, and used it as a bat to bash the potatoes with. 'SPLOSH'.... went one, 'SQUELCH' went another. 'SPLAT' and 'SPLOINK' they went, as Wika Waka fought them off.

Timmy-Trolley-Bus was laughing so hard he nearly fell out of the tree-house.

"Let us up," shouted Wika Waka.

"No! It's my tree-house now," laughed Timmy-Trolley-Bus.

Just then, as Wika Waka skillfully bashed another Dangerous Potato on the head, (BOINK) he had an idea. Some of the Potatoes were lying around, stunned. So Wika Waka picked one up, holding it firmly so it couldn't bite him. Then, standing at the bottom of the tree, he pushed the big red button on his training shoes. The shoes started to flash and whirrrr. To everyone's amazement, Wika Waka started to walk up the side of the tree, still holding the stunned Dangerous Potato. And do you know what? Timmy-Trolley-Bus wasn't laughing any more.

"What are you going to do with that potato?" he asked nervously, as Wika Waka stopped right next to the tree-house.

"It's a present for you," said Wika Waka teasingly. Then he lobbed the angry Dangerous Potato into the tree-house just like a hand-grenade, and listened for the telltale sound of a potato biting a bottom.

"YEEEEEEAAAAAAAAHHHHHHHHHHWWWWWWW," screamed Timmy-Trolley-Bus, as he wriggled around trying to pull the Potato off his bum. *"GET IT OFF! GET IT OFF!"* he screamed. But the potato was so angry at being hit on the head, it wasn't going to let go. Timmy-Trolley-Bus fell out of the tree-house into the middle of the horde of rabid, hungry Dangerous Potatoes. They bit him all over, and the naughty boy ran off into the night, with potatoes hanging off every part of him, especially his bottom.

"AAAAAAAAAHHHHHHHHHhhhhhhhhhhhh," he screamed, as he ran off into the distance.

Wika Waka scrambled into the tree-house and lowered the crane to winch up the trike, carrying Monkeyman and Squinkle. The children looked down at the raging sea of Dangerous Potatoes as they were lifted up to the safe vantage point of their tree-house. The three stood for a moment, too out of breath to speak, while the strange eerie howls echoed beneath them. Finally Monkeyman said, "Well, we know one thing for sure."

"What's that?" asked Wika Waka.

"The metal pants work!" and she held a big, broken, potato tooth up for them to see.

"Great. When do I get mine?" asked Squinkle, "I want to go potato-hunting."

The End